Pet Corner

COLORFUL GOLDFISH

By Katie Kawa

Gareth Stevens
Publishing

Please visit our website, www.garethstevens.com. For a free color catalog of all our high-quality books, call toll free 1-800-542-2595 or fax 1-877-542-2596.

Library of Congress Cataloging-in-Publication Data

Kawa, Katie.
Colorful goldfish / Katie Kawa.
 p. cm. — (Pet corner)
ISBN 978-1-4339-5599-0 (pbk.)
ISBN 978-1-4339-5600-3 (6-pack)
ISBN 978-1-4339-5597-6 (library binding)
1. Goldfish—Juvenile literature. I. Title.
SF458.G6K39 2011
639.3'7484—dc22
                                                  2010053769

First Edition

Published in 2012 by
Gareth Stevens Publishing
111 East 14th Street, Suite 349
New York, NY 10003

Copyright © 2012 Gareth Stevens Publishing

Editor: Katie Kawa
Designer: Andrea Davison-Bartolotta

Photo credits: Cover, pp. 1, 7, 11, 13, 17, 19, 21, 23, 24 (fins) Shutterstock.com; p. 5 iStockphoto.com; pp. 9, 24 (tank) Dorling Kindersley/Getty Images; p. 15 Zac Macaulay/Getty Images.

All rights reserved. No part of this book may be reproduced in any form without permission in writing from the publisher, except by a reviewer.

Printed in the United States of America

CPSIA compliance information: Batch #CS11GS: For further information contact Gareth Stevens, New York, New York at 1-800-542-2595.

Contents

Life in a Tank 4

Goldfish Care 12

Always Growing 20

Words to Know 24

Index. 24

Many goldfish are orange.

5

Goldfish are smart.
They know who takes care of them.

7

A goldfish lives in a fish tank.

9

The tank is big.
Goldfish need room
to grow.

11

Clean water goes in every week.

13

Goldfish eat fish food. The food sits on top of the water.

15

A goldfish has seven fins. These help it swim.

17

A goldfish sleeps. Its eyes stay open.

19

Some goldfish are
30 years old!

21

A goldfish never stops growing!

23

Words to Know

fins   tank

Index

fins 16   tank 8, 10
food 14   water 12, 14

24